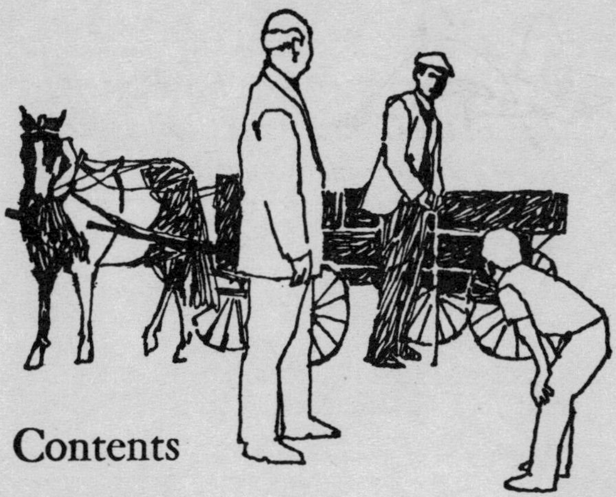

Contents

The Alden Family Mysteries
by Gertrude Chandler Warner

THE BOXCAR CHILDREN
SURPRISE ISLAND
THE YELLOW HOUSE MYSTERY
MYSTERY RANCH
MIKE'S MYSTERY
BLUE BAY MYSTERY
THE WOODSHED MYSTERY
THE LIGHTHOUSE MYSTERY
MOUNTAIN TOP MYSTERY
SCHOOLHOUSE MYSTERY
CABOOSE MYSTERY
HOUSEBOAT MYSTERY
SNOWBOUND MYSTERY
TREE HOUSE MYSTERY
BICYCLE MYSTERY
MYSTERY IN THE SAND
MYSTERY BEHIND THE WALL
BUS STATION MYSTERY
BENNY UNCOVERS A MYSTERY

Houseboat Mystery

GERTRUDE CHANDLER WARNER

Illustrated by David Cunningham

ALBERT WHITMAN & Company, Niles, Illinois

My thanks to
Commander Neal E. Williams
of the United States Coast Guard
for many courtesies.
G.C.W.

ISBN 0-8075-3413-7

9 11 13 15 17 18 16 14 12 10

Printed in the U.S.A.

CHAPTER 1

Houseboat for Rent

What a hot day in July! The four Alden children were sitting under the trees with their grandfather. This was the coolest place they could find.

"Oh, it's so hot!" said Benny Alden. "Let's go for a ride."

"Good!" said Grandfather Alden, looking at his four grandchildren. He stood up. "I was hoping somebody would have a good idea. Henry—"

But Henry, who was older than Benny, had gone. They could hear him in the garage getting out the station wagon.

Jessie wiped her face with a large handkerchief. "Let's ride until it gets cooler," she said. "The weather report says this heat is going to last for a week."

The Aldens' dog, Watch, wagged his tail as he lay at Jessie's feet. "Yes, Watch, you can go, too," Jessie said.

Watch gave a bark and trotted along with the family. They all walked across the grass to the drive. Violet put her arm through her grandfather's and said, "This family has the best ideas. Don't you think so, Grandfather?"

"Yes, indeed," Mr. Alden replied as he smiled at his younger granddaughter. "Somebody always thinks of something to do when we need it."

"It's funny," said Jessie. "Things always seem to happen to this family when we don't expect them. I was thinking I'd never feel cool again. But we will be cooler just as soon as the car is moving."

Henry stopped the car in the driveway. The children, Grandfather, and Watch all got in and away they went. Every window was open as they rode along a straight highway.

Henry said, "Benny, I'm glad you thought of this. I feel better already."

The Aldens rode for over an hour. Then Henry saw a sign at the left saying River Road. Henry turned left. Soon he was driving along a small river.

"Good," said Benny. "This is even cooler. And I don't think we've ever been here before."

Jessie said, "You don't have to drive so fast, Henry. My hair is blowing out straight."

It was a good thing that Henry slowed down. If he had not, the Alden family might have missed an exciting adventure. But no one guessed it then.

The pretty little river flowed slowly along. There were cool green banks and trees on both sides. All at once Henry slowed down still more.

"I hear whistling," he said. The family listened. They could hear it, too, down by the river.

Suddenly they came to a short side road that led to the river itself. Henry stopped the car, and they all looked down the side road.

"What in the world is that thing?" asked Benny. "Is it a boat?" He pointed to a little house that seemed to be sitting in the water.

"It's a houseboat, I do believe!" said Mr. Alden. "I haven't seen one for years and years."

"Let's drive down," said Henry. "We can see what's going on. My, this is a rough road! Lucky for me it is so short." Henry drove slowly down the rough side road to the edge of the river.

They all looked at the little house. It had four windows and two ladders which led to the roof. At one end was a blue awning that covered the front deck. A railing ran all the way around the boat. Another railing ran around the roof. On the lower deck of the houseboat a man was sitting in a chair, whistling.

"Hello, there!" he called. "Want to see the houseboat? My name is Rivers."

The family got out of the car and went down to see the strange man and the strange boat. The houseboat was anchored at a small dock, and also tied to the dock with a rope.

Benny looked at the dark blue letters on top of the boat. "Its name is *The Blue Heron*," he said. "How did you happen to name it that?"

"I didn't," said Mr. Rivers. "The couple who just left named it that. You see, the people who rent this boat can name it anything they like. Come on board, and I'll show you. Just step from the dock over here." He took off a chain to make an opening in the railing.

Watch began to whine. "Never mind, Watch," said Jessie. "You don't have to come. You just sit here and wait."

The Aldens stepped on board the houseboat, leaving Watch sitting on the dock.

Mr. Rivers took down a rack that was fastened against the wall.

"Here are all the letters of the alphabet," he said. "People who rent the boat pick out the letters and spell any name they like. You'd laugh at some of the names this boat has had. One couple named it *Rock and Roll*. Another named it *Moon Rocket*. And another tired family named it *The All Inn*."

Benny laughed. "It would be fun to name a boat," he said. "It could even be a different name every day. Now the first day we could name it for Grandfather, *The James H. Alden*. The next day it could be *The Henry James Alden*, then *The Jessie Alden*, and so on."

Everybody laughed. Mr. Rivers said, "I guess you're the one in the family with grand ideas. Comical, I'd say."

"Benny talks as if we were really going to rent your houseboat, Mr. Rivers," said Jessie. "And it really would be fun. There are chairs on the deck and everything. I suppose you can sit here under the awning and stay out of the hot sun."

Mr. Rivers smiled. He pointed to the flat roof of

the houseboat. "Yes, and if you want to get tanned, just climb up the ladder and lie down in the sun."

Violet said, "Just look at the pretty white curtains in the windows. They make it look like a big doll-house."

Mr. Alden had been looking at the houseboat, too, and now he looked at Mr. Rivers. He seemed to like what he saw. "Do you own this boat?" he asked.

"Yes, I do," Mr. Rivers answered. "I rent this boat by the week. Everybody seems to like it. The last family went today, and they were very sorry to go. I have just cleaned it all up for the next customer. Why don't you look around?"

"Oh, let's look at it, Grandfather," said Jessie.

"It's made like a flatboat," said Henry. He was looking down over the railing into the water. "It's like a raft. I'm sure it can't go very fast."

"That's right," said Mr. Rivers. "In fact, it just floats down the river all by itself. If you want to land, you can use those two poles to push it ashore. Coming back up the river, you have to use the motor on the back."

Grandfather said, "Well, this river seems to be

very slow. I must say that living here would be a nice quiet rest. Of course, these grandchildren of mine are all tired out by a whole year in school. They would just love to do nothing."

The Aldens looked at their grandfather. They knew he was joking because *no* Alden ever liked to do nothing.

"Let's go inside," said Jessie.

Benny was inside already. He sat on one of the bunk beds. "I don't think this boat is big enough for us, Mr. Rivers," he said. "We need five beds and there are only two."

"There are six beds," said Mr. Rivers, smiling.

"Where?" asked Benny. He looked all around, but he didn't see any more bunks.

Mr. Rivers said, "A houseboat has to be small. Everything has to be shipshape. That means that things must be in perfect order or you can't get everything in. Here are the other beds." He pulled one down out of the wall.

"What do you know!" said Benny. "That's pretty smart. Now I see the others. They all have curtains."

"I suppose this is the water tank under the sink,"

said Henry. He took off the cover. "You can't drink the river water, can you?"

"No, you have to go ashore for drinking water and supplies. There are many places along the river where you can stop for water and ice and other things. You can use the river water for washing, though."

"Let's go, Grandfather!" said Benny.

The Aldens knew what Benny meant. He wanted to rent the houseboat and start out tomorrow. That was how the Aldens liked to do things—in a hurry.

But Mr. Alden was not in a hurry this time. He put his hand on Benny's shoulder and said, "We'd better go slow, Benny. We have to know how to handle this boat for one thing."

"I know how," said Henry.

Everyone stared at him. "How do you know, Henry?" asked Benny.

"Well, you remember one weekend I visited a fellow in school? His family had a boat something like this, and I learned how to steer it. We had a grand time. Benny can help me pole the boat when we want to land, and I know how to run the outboard motor when we want to come home."

"Well, how lucky!" said Jessie. It was plain that she wanted to try living on the houseboat.

Violet said, "If we don't like it, we can always come back, can't we?"

That settled it for Mr. Alden. He really wanted to try it himself.

Mr. Rivers said, "It is really very safe. This river has no dangerous places. Every night it is easy to find a place along the bank to drop anchor. There aren't many boats on this river, but still you don't want one of them to run into you. Do you understand about lights, young man?"

"Yes," said Henry. "From sunset to sunrise there must be white lights about eight feet above the water so that other boats can see you for one mile."

"Well, well!" said Mr. Rivers. "Good for you! What else do you know?"

"I suppose you have a fire extinguisher and life jackets?" answered Henry. "And a bell? Yes, I see the bell right up there on top."

Mr. Rivers said, "Life jackets right there. Six of them." He pointed to the wall of the first cabin. "And it's the law to have a fire extinguisher. I have a fire pail and a sandbox, too. You know that you can put out a fire by pouring sand on it."

Benny got down and read the printing on the pail. It said, "Keep water up to this line." On the sandbox it said, "Keep sand up to this line."

Mr. Rivers explained, "We never had a fire yet. Everyone is careful. I had one family that let the baby play in the sand. I soon stopped that."

"You don't have to worry about us," said Benny. "We promise not to play in the sand. And besides, I lost my last pail and shovel a long time ago."

"You're good-natured," said Mr. Rivers. "You always see the funny side, don't you? Comical."

Benny looked at Henry and said, "I guess you should be the captain."

"Then you can be my first mate," said Henry.

Mr. Rivers said, "That's fine! This boat is registered with the Coast Guard. They know all about it, even when its name is something different."

"Oh, let's go!" said Benny.

"When?" asked Mr. Rivers.

"Tomorrow," said Grandfather, before Benny could answer. "We'll be here at ten o'clock."

Watch was whining and barking when his family stepped on the dock. "You don't like this, do you, old fellow?" Henry said to the dog. "Come and get in the car."

He turned the car around while Mr. Alden talked with Mr. Rivers about the rent.

"Here's the key," said Mr. Rivers. "Lock up at night. And whenever you go to the store, shut the windows, too. The windows lock themselves when you shut them."

The Aldens all were excited. They started up the rough side road, waving to Mr. Rivers. Grandfather gave the key to Henry. "Here, Captain," he said.

Mr. Rivers shouted after them, "Don't bring too many things!"

"No, we won't," Jessie called back. Then she said to her family, "We won't need many clothes. We can all just live in swimsuits and sweaters—all but Grandfather."

Grandfather winked at Benny. "You'd be surprised," he said.

Henry drove the car carefully up the rough side road and stopped before turning at River Road.

Suddenly, right in front of him, a heavy black car came roaring down River Road. It turned a sharp corner past Henry, down the side road toward the houseboat. Stones flew as the tires screamed and the car skidded past the Aldens' station wagon. It almost hit it.

"Hey! What are they thinking of?" said Henry.

"Whew!" said Benny. "Those two men almost hit us! That was a close one!"

Violet said, "What in the world do they want of a houseboat? People who drive like that?"

Nobody felt much like talking. Henry started slowly down River Road toward home. He looked in his rearview mirror. "Here are our friends again," he said. He pulled over to the right and slowed down. The black car roared past.

Henry said, "Well, what's their hurry? What do they want with our houseboat, anyway?"

Benny said, "I guess they don't want it. They didn't stay long enough even to look at it. I hope we won't ever see them again."

Henry wondered, but he said nothing.

CHAPTER 2

Henry's Invention

The next morning Henry said, "I have to leave half this stuff at home. I've got to take my camera and a flashlight and my fishing rod and tackle."

"Can't take that fishing tackle, Henry," called Mr. Alden from his room. "This time we will have to go without some things. There isn't room on the boat."

Jessie said, "Henry, I'm afraid Watch thinks he is going. It's too bad to leave him at home." She looked at the big dog lying right in the way. She stepped over him.

Benny said, "He wouldn't like a houseboat trip. He whined when we went aboard. He would bark every time we went swimming. You'll be better off at home, Watch, with Mrs. McGregor."

When the Aldens were away, Mrs. McGregor, their housekeeper, took care of things. She nodded and said, "Watch is always all right after you go. He sleeps in the hall and wags his tail when I go by. Then he walks out in the yard and lies in the shade. Don't worry about him."

At last the Aldens had everything stuffed into their suitcases. Henry had his camera and Benny had a flashlight.

Mrs. McGregor was right. Watch barked a little, but not much. He sat on the front steps with Mrs. McGregor as the Aldens packed the car.

When Henry drove away, Jessie looked back and saw Watch go into the house with Mrs. McGregor. He didn't even try to follow the car.

"Well," Jessie said, "we don't have to worry about Watch anymore. I'm glad."

When the Aldens reached River Road, Mr. Alden said, "There is a store on this road before we get to the houseboat."

"Yes, Mr. Rivers told me about it, too," said Jessie.

"He says all the houseboat people get their food there. The man knows what they need."

As the Aldens came into the store, the groceryman said, "So you want to try houseboat life?"

"That's right," Benny said.

"Five of you, I see," said the man. "You can choose between three cans of tuna and three cans of chicken. Take two cans of beans or two cans of hash. You can use a dozen eggs, two quarts of milk, two loaves of bread, sugar, salt, and butter. One cake of soap can be used for washing everything."

"Coffee?" asked Violet, looking at Grandfather.

"Oh, yes, coffee," the groceryman said. "But if you forget anything, you can stop and buy more down the river. We call it Second Landing."

The Aldens put the groceries in the car and went along toward the houseboat. Mr. Rivers was there.

"Right on time!" he said. "You can lock your car and park it here. It will be safe. I'll help you unload."

"Fine!" said Benny. "I can hardly wait to see this boat go."

"You can hardly see it go," said Mr. Rivers, "even when it goes." That made everyone laugh.

The suitcases and supplies were soon on board. Benny climbed up the ladder and changed the name to *The James H. Alden*.

"Looks fine," said Mr. Rivers. Then he said to Henry, "Just pole yourself out to the middle of the river. It's about eight feet deep. You can dive out there all right."

"This is so exciting," said Jessie as Henry pulled up the anchor and Mr. Rivers untied the rope.

Henry began to pole. Then suddenly there they were, floating gently away!

"Goody-bye, Mr. Rivers!" they shouted.

"Good luck!" he called. He watched them as they went out of sight around a bend in the river.

"Oh, let's just watch the river for a little while," said Violet. She sat down on the deck. "It won't take us long to get settled."

It was peaceful on the river. Sometimes it was so narrow that the beautiful trees almost met overhead. A big orange-and-black butterfly flew right across the deck.

"Look, a milkweed butterfly," said Violet.

Benny looked at the cattails. They grew very thick

near the shore. Suddenly he pointed. A red-winged blackbird was swinging on the reeds.

"Isn't that beautiful?" said Jessie. "What bright red and yellow on his black wings!"

"He doesn't sing," said Violet. "Oh, he saw us. Do you suppose he has a nest somewhere?"

Then they all saw the nest. A dull brown bird flew off, showing a grassy cup with five blue eggs in it.

Mr. Alden said, "This must be their second family this year. It is too late for the first one."

Benny said, "That pattern on the eggs is like modern art. All those brown wiggles. And look—there's a blue heron."

The water bird stood on one leg and did not move. He was so near that the Aldens could see every blue-gray feather and its black eyes.

"That's probably why that other family named this boat *The Blue Heron*," said Benny. "Maybe they saw a lot of blue herons."

In a little while the Aldens began to put things away. Jessie put the food on the shelf. She came back on the deck to get the box of salt. Just as she picked it up, a bird flew right in front of her.

"Oh!" cried Jessie, jumping back. The salt slipped out of her hand and rolled along the deck, over the edge, and into the water.

"Oh, how could I?" said Jessie. "Now we haven't any salt. And we must have salt."

Grandfather said, "Don't worry, Jessie. We'll just watch for Second Landing and get another box of salt."

In about half an hour Benny called out, "There it is. That must be Second Landing."

"Yes," said Henry. "And it looks as if there are several buildings there."

Henry poled *The James H. Alden* up to the dock. The Aldens remembered what Mr. Rivers had said. They locked the houseboat, windows and all. Henry made sure it was tied up safely and the anchor dropped.

As usual, Benny was in a hurry. He was the first one on the dock and the first one on the narrow path. As he went through the bushes, he didn't see a stone in his way and tripped over it and fell. When he stood up, he was covered with dirt and grass stains.

Jessie brushed him off and said, "Well, I guess I'll

have to wash these clothes, Ben. When we get back to the houseboat, you pull up a pail of water from the river."

Violet added, "You can put on your swimsuit while your clothes dry. We can hang them on that little clothesline on the houseboat."

"Oh," said Benny, "that's a lot of work. I don't care much how I look."

"Yes, Ben, we know that," said Henry with a smile.

"There's your store," said Benny, pointing. A sign said, "Eric A. Martin, Groceries."

The whole family went into the store. "I need a box of salt," Jessie told the man behind the counter. "Ours rolled overboard."

The man laughed and took some salt off the shelf. "Are you the folks in the Rivers houseboat?" he asked.

"That's right," said Violet. "How did you guess?"

"Almost everyone forgets something or loses something," said Mr. Martin. "They come in here because it's the first place to stop."

Henry asked, "Do you have any clothesline?"

Everybody stared at Henry. Jessie said, "There's a fine clothesline on the boat, Henry."

Mr. Martin said, "Yes, I have two kinds. Cotton and plastic."

"I think I want cotton," said Henry. "It's softer."

"Yes, it is softer and it stretches more," Mr. Martin agreed.

"Good," said Henry, looking at the bunch of line. "Not too many feet in one bunch. I'll have to take two. I want a ball of string, too, please."

"What in the world do you want with two bunches of clothesline and a ball of string?" asked Jessie.

"Secret," replied Henry. "I don't want to tell because I may not have good luck."

"Oh, you will, Henry," said Benny. "I know you. You must have a secret idea."

"Let's buy some bananas," said Jessie. "They're a good dessert, and there's no cooking."

Mr. Martin nodded. "Yes, you must have everything shipshape on a boat. You can't cook too many things."

Violet was looking out of the window. She said,

"Grandfather, there's a restaurant on the other side of the street."

"It's a good one, too," said Mr. Martin. "Very good food."

Violet went on, "It's almost noon. I think it would save time to eat lunch here. We have so much to do on the boat."

"Good!" said Grandfather. "We'll do that."

The Aldens said good-bye to Mr. Martin and walked across the street with their groceries.

There were only two men in the restaurant, having lunch. They sat off in one corner. The Aldens sat down at a big table on the other side of the room.

The food was excellent, and they all chose ice cream for dessert.

"No ice cream for a while," said Jessie. "It won't stay frozen on a houseboat."

Benny and Grandfather were facing the two men. Benny looked at them and decided he didn't like them. He didn't really know why, so he said nothing.

Mr. Alden looked at the strangers, too. He thought, "I wonder what they are talking about. It seems to be nothing good."

This was such a small restaurant that a husband and wife ran it alone. The man was the cook and his wife was the waitress.

Benny noticed the woman as she came out of the kitchen. She went over to the table where the two men sat. She asked, "Do you want more coffee?"

One of the men said, "Yes, I'd like some more."

But when the waitress put down the cup, Benny saw her slip a small envelope under the saucer. Then

she looked back toward the kitchen where her husband was. But the man was too busy to notice. He went on cooking.

The man at the table put the envelope into his pocket and tried to smile at the woman. But it was not a real smile. The waitress walked quickly over to the Aldens' table.

The men kept their heads down as they talked in low voices. When the Aldens started to go out, Benny heard one man say roughly to the other, "What do you mean—find out? Nobody has found out yet. And it's three years."

When the Aldens were in the street, Benny said, "I don't like those men in there."

Henry looked at his brother and said, "What's the matter, Ben? You always like everybody."

"Well, I don't like them," said Benny. "That's for sure. You were sitting with your back to them. You didn't see them. What do you think, Grandfather?"

"I agree with you perfectly, Benny," said Mr. Alden. "I didn't like them either. They are up to no good."

"Well, we'll never see them again," said Jessie,

"and I'm glad."

The Aldens started back toward the houseboat. Benny looked back at the restaurant and stopped suddenly. He could just see the front part of an expensive black car parked a little beyond the restaurant.

"I've seen that car before," Benny thought to himself. Then he knew! It was the heavy black car that had almost hit them the day before!

"Two men in a hurry," he thought. He decided to say nothing right away.

By now the Aldens had reached the houseboat. "It seems like home already," said Violet.

Benny said, "Now don't drop the salt again, Jessie."

Jessie got the salt safely aboard. Benny carried the clothesline and string for Henry. Mr. Alden and Henry untied the boat, and Henry poled it out into the middle of the stream. It floated beautifully, and yet it went slowly.

Benny asked Henry, "Are you going to tell your secret now, Henry?"

"No, but I'm going to work on it. We'll need it very soon. You can guess if you want to."

Just then Jessie said, "Benny, change your clothes and I'll wash your things out."

"Oh, let's watch Henry first," Benny answered.

Jessie herself wanted to watch when Henry brought his clothesline on the deck and began to measure it. He made many long loops. Then he laid the middle of each loop on the deck and crossed it with another rope. He tied this place together with string.

"What in the world!" said Violet. "Are you making a chair seat?"

Henry looked at his sister in astonishment. "How did you ever guess?" he said. "It doesn't look like anything so far."

"You mean I'm right?" asked Violet. "I was only guessing."

"Well, you guessed right," said Henry. He crossed another line and tied it.

"Why do we need another chair seat?" asked Benny. "We've got enough chairs, and someone can always lie down."

"This is different," said Henry. He tied the last cord. What he had made looked like a square piece of net with very long ends. "Remember that big hook on the back of the boat? But wait. I'll put on my swimming trunks first. You change, too, Benny."

When the boys came back, the family went down to the rear deck. Henry hung the loops on the hook so that the seat was over the water. He made a fine dive off the boat. He swam back and came up beside the new chair seat.

But when Henry got into the seat, it began to go down, down, down! The ropes stretched so much that Henry was soon up to his neck in water.

Everyone began to laugh. "A joke on me," said Henry. "I thought I could sit in this seat and wash Benny's clothes. Then we wouldn't have to take all that water on board."

"It's a good idea, though," said Mr. Alden quickly. "Maybe you can still make it work. Make the loops shorter."

"You're too heavy, Henry," said Benny.

Then Violet said, "Maybe I'm not. Let me do the laundry!" She went inside and put on her swimsuit. Henry climbed out of the seat and Violet climbed in. There she sat, just up to her waist in the river.

"Good for you," said Mr. Alden. "Too bad there isn't any laundry."

"Oh, but there is," said Violet. "Benny, just hand down your shirt and shorts and the cake of soap."

"You can't hold the soap," called Benny. "What will you do with it?"

"Well," said Violet looking around at the water, "put the soap dish on the deck and I'll put the soap in it every time I use it."

She soaped Benny's clothes and rubbed and rinsed them in the river.

"Pass them up to me, Violet," said Jessie. "I'll hang them on the real clothesline. There's nothing so homelike as having washing on the line."

Then they all went swimming. The water was cool and lovely. Even Mr. Alden was floating beside the boat.

"This is the nicest place," said Benny. "If you want to go swimming, just jump out the window."

After their swim, the Aldens were glad to sit on the deck. Everyone was so hungry that they had supper at five o'clock.

Henry took his last bite and said, "I think we

should find a place for the night before it gets any darker."

"You and Benny find one," said Jessie. "Violet and I will wash the dishes and clean up the kitchen."

"Galley, not kitchen," said Mr. Alden. And after that it was always the galley.

The boys found a fine place to stay for the night, where the branches of the trees hung over the houseboat. They left the windows open, but locked the doors.

In his bunk, Benny turned this way and that. He could not get to sleep. He kept remembering those two men in the restaurant and the little envelope and the big black car parked outside.

CHAPTER 3

Trouble Brewing

The first morning on *The James H. Alden* was bright and sunny. As soon as Benny was dressed he climbed up the ladder to change the name of the boat to *The Henry J. Alden.*

"This boat is all yours, captain," he called to Henry as he came down again.

Henry went out on the deck to look. He began to laugh. "You did well, mate," Henry said. "Come and see for yourself."

Benny looked up and began to laugh, too. The name was *nedlA .J yrneH ebT!*

"Well, it looked okay to me," Benny said, climbing up the ladder again. "But it's backwards to everyone else." He soon changed the letters to read the right way.

Jessie was in the galley looking out the window. "It's so cool and pleasant on this boat," she said. "I suppose it's because we're on the water. Oh, the boat is moving sideways!"

"Don't worry, Jessie," said Henry. "Mr. Rivers said it doesn't do any harm. The boat will straighten out by itself or I can pole it back."

Henry did not need to pole the houseboat. It soon turned slowly by itself.

Henry went inside the cabin. He looked up and said, "Look, there's a fishing pole up there and a fishnet with a long handle. I think I'll go fishing."

"Not a very good day for fishing, Henry," said Benny. "The sun is too bright."

"It's okay, Ben," said Henry. "I think I'll try my luck anyway." Henry took down the pole and fishnet and looked at the line and hook.

"What are you going to use for bait, Henry?" asked Benny.

"Oh, I don't know," said Henry. "This is one time I have to use what we've got."

Benny thought a minute. Then he said, "Didn't we see a lot of little minnows yesterday? Maybe we could catch some of them in that net."

"Good for you, Ben!" said Henry. "Minnows are the best bait of all. They swim near the shore, where the water isn't so deep. I'll pole in nearer."

Both boys began to pole. When they reached shallow water, they looked over the side. Sure enough, they saw hundreds of minnows swimming around.

"This is easy!" said Benny. He bent over with the net and pulled up a lot of the tiny fish.

"Now we're all set," said Henry. He poled back into the deeper water. He set two chairs on the rear deck. Then he put a tiny minnow on his hook. He threw the fishline out over the water and sat down with the heavy pole. Benny sat down beside him. The boat floated gently along. Everything was quiet.

Grandfather and Violet went out to the front deck. They smiled at each other. Violet said, "I wouldn't count on having fish for lunch today."

Mr. Alden nodded. "I'm afraid you're right if you mean fish from the river. But Jessie can give us tuna fish."

Just then Jessie came out on the deck to watch the river with Violet and Grandfather.

"This is the most peaceful trip we've ever had," Jessie said.

Mr. Alden, sitting in a deck chair, said, "Yes, it is."

A half hour passed.

Benny chattered away to his brother. The sun shone hotter than ever. Nothing happened. Not one fish had pulled at Henry's line.

"I was afraid of this," said Henry. "I'm not even sure there are any fish in this river."

"There must be some fish, Henry," said Benny. "If there weren't any, this boat wouldn't have had a fishing pole on it. I wish we had two poles."

"Here, Benny, you take this one," said Henry. He handed the pole to his brother. "We can take turns catching nothing."

Benny took the pole. He could see the line and the minnow still in the water.

Jessie and Violet came over to see how the fishing was going. They were both smiling.

Benny turned around with a frown on his face. "We're not doing too well," he said. "But you have to have patience when you're fishing." Then suddenly something pulled at his line.

"I've got you, old boy!" he called to the fish. He pulled in the line and found a big silver fish caught on the hook.

"A bass!" said Henry. "Don't lose him, Ben! He can flop back."

Benny was quick. He jerked the fish over the railing and it lay on the deck, flapping wildly. Suddenly a great cloud of gulls flew over the boat, calling and screaming.

"You can't have my fish!" Benny shouted to the birds. "How did you find out I caught a fish, anyway?"

It was a real mystery. One minute not a gull was in sight. The next minute, there were over a hundred. Gulls sat on the top of the boat and along the sides. They were not a bit afraid. They flew around and around looking for food.

Benny carried his fish safely inside the galley.

Jessie said, "The gulls are so beautiful. It's too bad not to feed them. Wait. Here's a piece of banana skin. They might like that." She threw it over the water as

far as she could. A gull caught it in his bill. She threw another.

Henry laughed, "Well, I guess gulls will eat anything."

Benny brought some bread crusts out of the galley. Each time he threw one over the side of the boat, a gull snapped it up before it landed in the water.

Henry went inside and came out with his camera. "That ought to make a pretty picture," he said. "You two pretty girls throwing rubbish at the gulls."

They all laughed.

When Henry looked at Benny's fish, he said, "It's a big bass. It is plenty big enough to feed this family. I'll clean it for you, Ben. The gulls can have the head and tail for dessert."

After a delicious lunch, Jessie said, "Oh, dear! We'll have to stop again for ice and milk."

Mr. Alden said, "I want to mail my letters, too."

Henry began to watch for a landing place.

At Pomfret Landing Jessie said, "Let's go to the post office first and get the ice and milk last. Then the ice won't melt."

The Henry J. Alden was soon locked up, anchored, and tied. The family walked down the path from the dock to the small town.

All at once they saw a familiar black car roaring down the main street. It was soon out of sight.

"It's that black car again!" Benny cried. The Aldens saw that it was the same car that had almost hit their car on River Road. And Benny remembered that he had seen it parked near the restaurant where they had stopped for lunch the day before.

"Whoever drives that car always seems to be in such a hurry!" said Jessie.

"I wonder whose car it is," said Henry. "It certainly doesn't belong in a small town like Pomfret Landing."

"Well, maybe we can find out just who does own that car," Grandfather said.

The Aldens walked up the main street to the post office. As they opened the door, the man behind the counter was saying, "Here's your stamp, Mrs. Young."

The little lady, who was wearing a black dress, put down her money and took the stamp.

The Aldens watched politely, but the lady did not

look up. She slipped out of the door like a shadow.

Mr. Alden bought a sheet of airmail stamps, some stamped envelopes, and some postcards.

Benny said, "I guess the lady who just left doesn't write many letters. She only bought one stamp."

"That's right," said the clerk. "Mrs. Young isn't exactly poor, but she has a lot of trouble. She and her son live with her sister up the street. They own a candy store."

"We'd better go and buy some candy," said Henry.

"You'll have to eat it now," said Jessie. "There's no place to put candy on the boat."

"You're from the Rivers' houseboat, aren't you?" asked the clerk, smiling.

"How do you know?" asked Benny.

"Oh, all the people from the houseboat come here," said the man. "We like to meet new people. Pomfret Landing is such a small place that we know everybody's business, I guess."

"We just saw an enormous black car go by," said Benny. "Who owns that?"

"I don't know," said the clerk, laughing. "That's

the only thing I don't know. I've seen it before, but it certainly doesn't belong in Pomfret Landing."

The Aldens left the post office and walked up the street to the candy store. As they went in, a bell on the door rang.

"Oh, isn't this a lovely store!" said Violet.

The wallpaper was white with pink stripes. The ruffled curtains were white with pink dots. Two small tables and some chairs stood by a tiny soda counter. The shelves were covered with lace paper. Boxes of candy were everywhere.

The store was empty, but soon a lady appeared. It was the same Mrs. Young. She now wore an apron over her black dress, and she looked more tired than ever. Jessie thought to herself, "She looks as if she has been crying."

Mrs. Young was trying to smile now as she said, "I'm glad you like my store. People come here from miles around."

"Do you make your own candy?" asked Mr. Alden.

"Well, my sister is really the candymaker," answered Mrs. Young. "But I help."

Benny looked at Mrs. Young with a bright smile. He said, "I've always wanted to know how they made those curly things on the top of the chocolates. Do you know?"

"I do, indeed," she replied. "Would you like to see it done? My sister is putting on those curly tails right now."

"What luck!" said Benny. "I certainly would."

Henry whispered to Jessie, "That Ben can get away with anything!"

Mrs. Young pushed back a curtain and led them all into the candy kitchen.

Mrs. Young's sister was standing over a pan of chocolate. She had gray hair and was older than Mrs. Young, but she had a tired and worried look, just like her sister.

The Aldens watched her as she worked. She took a pink center on a fork, dipped it into the melted chocolate, and set the piece of candy on some waxed paper. Then with a flip of her fork she laid the curly tail across the top.

"Oh, Violet!" said Jessie. "Wouldn't that be fun? Let's try it sometime. I never knew how it was done."

The centers were pink, white, yellow, pale green, and lavender. The sister smiled at Violet and said, "Your name is Violet? Here is a good one for you." She picked up a lavender center, covered it with chocolate, and put on the tail. "You will have to wait for it to cool before you eat it," the lady said.

"Oh, thank you," said Violet.

"How about a milk shake while we wait?" asked Mr. Alden.

Mrs. Young smiled again. "You'll like our milk shakes. We make our own syrup."

Jessie led the way back to the tables. She said, "This is a good idea. We can take our dessert home inside us this time."

The milk shakes were delicious.

Mr. Alden said, "Mine tastes exactly like fresh strawberries."

"It ought to," said Mrs. Young. "The strawberries grow in our backyard."

The Aldens did buy some candy, but it was not chocolate. It was too hot on the boat for chocolate. But Mrs. Young gave Violet hers, and one for each of the rest.

As the Aldens were leaving, Benny turned to Mrs. Young and said, "When we came down the street, we saw an enormous black car going very fast. Do you happen to know who owns it?"

To his surprise, Mrs. Young turned very red and looked more worried than ever. Indeed she turned away, saying, "I'm sure it doesn't belong in this town."

"Oh, I'm awfully sorry," said Benny. "It's none of my business."

"It's all right," said Mrs. Young. "Come again." Then nobody heard what she said, because she almost whispered the words. Jessie heard the word "worried" but that was all.

When the Aldens were halfway down the street, Benny said, "I didn't mean to upset her. I just thought she might know who was driving that car."

Violet said softly, "I think she does."

That night Benny was just floating off to sleep. He was almost dreaming. But suddenly he heard Mrs. Young's words very plainly, "I'm just worried about my boy."

Boy? What boy? Then Benny was asleep.

CHAPTER 4

The Auction

The next morning Benny climbed up to the roof of the houseboat. He called down to Jessie, "Look here and see if I have the new name right."

"Oh, this is my day!" Jessie said, as she read *The Jessie Alden*. "I like having a houseboat named for me."

Henry asked, "Do you need to buy food today? Benny and I can watch for a place to land."

"No," said Jessie, shaking her head. "I have plenty of food for another day. We can just enjoy house-boating." She looked up at the trees. "See, the branches almost meet over our heads. Isn't it beautiful?"

The Aldens sat in chairs on the deck and watched the river grow wider and then narrower. Suddenly Jessie said, "Look, Grandfather! See that sign on the bank of the river? It says there's an auction!"

The sign did indeed say:

AUCTION, EVERY SATURDAY AT 10 A.M.

"Oh, you love auctions, Grandfather!" said Violet. "Let's stop."

Grandfather said, "You're right, Violet. I do love auctions. But do you all want to go?"

Benny looked at his grandfather and said, "I never went to an auction in my whole life!"

"Neither did I," said Violet.

Mr. Alden said, "I can't believe it! I know it is so, but I can't understand why I never took you to an auction."

"You took me once," said Henry. "And Jessie went, too. But that was years ago. Benny and Violet would love it, that's for sure. It's exciting, Ben."

Jessie said, "Some auctions are better than others. This auction must have some good things, if they have one every week."

Henry went on, "The auctioneer is very funny

sometimes. He tries to keep everybody good-natured. You see, Ben, people call out what they will pay for a clock or a rug. The one who pays the most gets it."

"That would be fun," said Benny. "Let's go."

"We're always saying 'Let's go!' " said Jessie, laughing.

Henry said, "Just give me time to lock the doors and shut the windows." They never forgot.

Henry and Benny poled the boat to the dock and anchored it and tied it.

When the Aldens reached the main street, they saw crowds of people going into a low, brown building with an enormous door. The door was as wide as the front of the building. The Aldens went along with the crowd.

Inside, they saw rows of folding chairs on the wooden floor. There was a little platform in the front, and on it were all sorts of things to sell. Furniture of all kinds stood on the platform. There were radios, TV sets, and bicycles. There were silver teapots, pictures of all sizes, and even baseball gloves. On a table was a box of old clothes and boxes of tin dishes and china and glass. It was fascinating.

Grandfather had seen many auctions. He always went up to the front seat. But this time, nobody seemed to be sitting down. All the people were up at the front of the hall, pushing and looking over the things to be sold. Some of the people had come to buy a book or a clock or a table for themselves. But dealers were there, too. They were men who bought things at an auction to sell again at a higher price. Dealers often bought furniture or dishes for their customers who had ordered them.

"Let's look around," said Benny. "It isn't ten o'clock yet."

"Then start here at the left end of the platform," said Mr. Alden, "and work toward the right. Then we'll see everything."

Grandfather looked at a few things. "There are some expensive things here," he said. "I wonder if there is a policeman around to see that nothing is stolen?"

"There's one over there," said Henry, pointing to a man standing in a corner. "But there are so many people here he can't watch everybody."

The crowd was good-natured. A big man laughed

and said to Henry, "Excuse me for pushing. I can't help it because someone is pushing me."

"That's all right," said Henry. "I'm pushing, too!"

There were children in the crowd. The boys were looking at the baseball suits and bats. Girls were looking at sweaters.

"That is a beautiful mirror," said Mr. Alden to Jessie. "And that desk is a very fine one, but—"

Someone pushed between Jessie and Grandfather, and Mr. Alden could not finish his sentence. When Jessie could get near him again, she asked, "What were you going to say, Grandfather?"

"I was going to say that the little vase way back on the desk is worth more than the desk."

Again Jessie was pushed a little way from Mr. Alden, but she called to him, "Let's stay right through this auction, Grandfather! We can eat lunch afterward. I'm sure we can find a restaurant."

"Just as you like," Mr. Alden called back.

Everyone nearby could hear all this. A lady turned to Mr. Alden and said, "There is a fine place right on Main Street called the Elm Tree Inn. There is a large elm tree right by the doorstep."

"Thank you!" said Mr. Alden. "We'll certainly go there."

Just then a bell rang. Everyone began to rush for seats. The Aldens found seats in the front row. Henry sat beside a man in a gray suit.

The auctioneer began. He held up a small painting.

"What am I offered?" he called out. "This is a hand-painted picture of the river."

A very young voice answered, "One dollar!"

Grandfather looked back to see who was bidding. It was a young boy, younger than Benny. Mr. Alden whispered to Henry, "It's a young boy in a red cap. He's very young to bid at an auction. He seems to be all alone."

The man in the gray suit called out, "Five dollars!"

"Six dollars!" called a woman's voice.

"Seven dollars!" said the man in the gray suit.

Grandfather whispered again to Henry, "I think that man beside you is a dealer. He knows what things are worth."

"Ten dollars!" called the woman.

The dealer said to Henry, "Oh, let her have it! It isn't worth more than ten dollars. They always start with the cheap things. I'm waiting for that little vase. It is out of sight now on the old desk."

"Yes, I saw that vase," said Henry.

The woman came forward and took the painting and gave the man ten dollars.

Then the auctioneer held up a box of old clothes. He took a boy's shirt off the top and held it up. He said, "There are five shirts in this box, a boy's jacket, a man's heavy overcoat, and five women's dresses. What am I offered?"

"One dollar!" called the boy in the red cap.

"Two dollars!" called a man.

"Three dollars!" called the boy.

"Four dollars!" shouted another man.

"Five dollars!" called the boy.

There was no answer. Nobody would bid higher than that.

"Going, going, gone!" said the auctioneer. "To the boy in the red cap!"

The boy came forward and took the box. He gave the man five one-dollar bills. Everyone smiled at the boy as he went out with the box of old clothes. He looked very much pleased with the things he had bought.

Benny whispered to Henry, "I saw that boy in the red cap looking over that box. I guess he is poor."

"Well, he had five dollars, Ben," said Henry. "And he got what he wanted. He's gone, anyway."

Benny half stood up. He looked through the window after the boy. He was surprised when he saw the boy begin to run. The boy was soon out of sight.

"That's funny," thought Benny. "I wonder why he was in such a hurry. Maybe he wants to show the things to his mother."

At last the cheaper things were sold. The expensive things would be put up for sale now. The crowd began to talk and buzz. They made a great noise in their excitement.

"Quiet!" said the auctioneer.

First the dealer in the gray suit bought an old table for $500. He laughed as he paid for it. He knew he could sell it for more. But when he came back to his seat, he said to Henry, "I'm really waiting for that vase."

At last the auctioneer came to the vase. He said to the crowd, "The vase I am going to sell next is the best piece here. It is very old and made of gold. You see! A rhyme! Old and gold."

The people laughed.

Then the auctioneer went on, "This vase has rubies and emeralds set in the gold. It came from Egypt. I am talking about this small vase on the desk."

He turned to take the vase off the desk, but the vase was not there!

The dealer whispered, "Stolen! I bet it was stolen!"

It seemed that the dealer was right. The vase could not be found. Again the crowd began to buzz.

"I stood right here," said the policeman. "But I didn't see anyone take it."

"Well, somebody took it," said the auctioneer.

"Too bad," said Grandfather. "Let's go. This auction is no fun anymore. No one likes to think there is a thief in the room."

"Yes, you can go," said the policeman to Grandfather. "I'm sure you didn't take the vase."

"I should say not," said Grandfather. "I know the police will take care of this."

Indeed, as the Aldens went out of the building, they met two more policemen coming in. Henry thought, "Someone must have telephoned the police station."

As he passed a policeman on the steps, Benny said to him, "I hope you will find that vase."

"Oh, we'll find it," the policeman answered.

"There are strange things going on around here. This is only one of them."

The other policeman added, "Right up and down our own river! It always has been so peaceful here. Nothing like this ever happened before."

The Aldens went along the street looking for the Elm Tree Inn. It was easy to find, for they soon saw the big tree.

Violet said, "I don't feel very hungry. But we'd better eat just the same, I suppose."

Jessie smiled and said, "We've got a chance now to eat without cooking a meal or washing the dishes. We'd better eat whether we're hungry or not."

"Well, I'm hungry," said Benny.

"So am I, mate," said Henry. "It will be no trouble at all for me."

Benny held the door of the Elm Tree Inn open while the others went in. Just as he was going to follow them he looked toward the street. He was in time to see a big black car swing out to pass a small truck. The truck driver called out, "Hey! Look where you're going!"

Benny had a fine chance to see the driver of the

black car as it whizzed by. He thought to himself, "That is the very man I saw in the restaurant! He's the one I didn't like. He's the one who said, 'What do you mean—find out? Nobody has found out yet.' "

The driver's left hand was on the small open window of the black car. He drove with his right hand. Benny saw that the man wore a big square black ring. Then the car was around the corner and out of sight. Benny went into the inn.

The family stayed a long time at the Elm Tree Inn. The restaurant was crowded with people. The waitress could not serve them for a long time. But as they waited for their lunch, Benny told them in a low voice about the man in the car.

Then Jessie said, "Those men don't seem to do anything wrong. They just drive too fast."

"Well, they almost ran into our car," said Henry. "I won't forget that in a hurry."

By the time the food was served, every Alden was hungry. Even Violet ate an excellent meal.

After lunch, Violet said, "Let's go, Grandfather. I'm tired."

Everyone agreed. They all wanted to get back to

the houseboat.

As the family walked along, Henry said, "I wonder what those policemen meant about strange things. Maybe that black car has something to do with all the trouble. It certainly looks strange in these small towns. It goes too fast."

Violet said, "Maybe the police have seen those two men who almost ran into us."

"I don't like them," said Benny. "I didn't like them when I saw them in the restaurant."

The Aldens walked down the path. They found the houseboat still safely anchored at the dock. Benny untied the rope, and Henry unlocked the door. They all went into the cabin.

Everyone began to sniff.

"Smoke!" said Benny. "I smell smoke! Where's that sandbox? I want that sand ready if there's a fire."

"It's cigarette smoke," said Henry. "No fire."

Grandfather looked very sober. He said, "Henry, unlock the back door, too. You can use the same key."

Grandfather looked at both doors. Then he tried the windows. They were all locked.

Jessie looked around the galley. Not a dish had been moved. Violet looked at the beds and the curtains.

Henry went out and checked the motor. It seemed to be all right.

They looked in the icebox and even in the water tank. They could not find a thing.

"I don't like it," said Grandfather. "Both doors were locked, and there isn't a mark on the keyholes."

After a while they all agreed on one thing—someone had been in the cabin, smoking a cigarette.

Benny said, "You know, this was a fine time for someone to get into this houseboat. Everybody at that auction knew we were going to eat lunch on land. Remember, Jessie, how you called to Grandfather?"

Jessie nodded. "And a stranger even said, 'I know a place where you can eat—the Elm Tree Inn.' Oh, yes, I guess we told everybody in that town that we wouldn't be home for a while."

Benny went out on the front deck and sat down to think. He was thinking about the boy in the red cap. It was strange how he ran away from the auction.

"Something funny here," Benny said to himself.

"But that boy is too young to be smoking cigarettes. Besides, he seemed like such a nice boy. I liked him the minute I saw him looking over the box of old clothes."

Everyone came out on the front deck and sat down.

Henry said, "Whoever was in our houseboat wasn't very smart. Anyone would know we would smell smoke. How do you think the person got in, Grandfather?"

Mr. Alden answered, "Well, I think someone has a key."

Benny was safely in bed that night. Suddenly he felt that something was missing. Then he knew what it was. He could not hear the clock tick! He looked out in the dark and found the spot on the wall where the clock hung. The clock was gone!

"Now I know someone has been here," Benny thought. "I know people often steal clocks and radios because they can sell them. But I wouldn't think anyone would come aboard just for a little old clock."

Benny did not want to wake everybody up to tell them, so he turned over and went to sleep.

CHAPTER 5

April Center

The day came when Benny changed the name of the houseboat to *The Watch Alden.* The family spent the morning cleaning up the boat and doing the laundry. After lunch, the four young Aldens were sitting on the front deck. Suddenly they saw a large sign on the riverbank. Benny read it aloud, April Center. "What does that mean?" he asked. "There's a dock and everything."

Mr. Alden, who was sitting in the cabin, heard Benny. He came out at once and looked at the sign.

"It can't be! It simply can't be!" he said.

"What can't be?" asked Henry and Benny.

"Well, April Center," answered Mr. Alden, still

staring at the sign. "That belongs to my old friend, George April."

"That's a funny name," said Benny. "Mr. April."

"I suppose so," said Grandfather. "I have known George April for years and years. He lives in London now."

"What is this April Center?" asked Henry.

Grandfather seemed to wake out of a daze. "Oh, yes, Henry! It's Mr. April's idea. He is interested in old things and new things—he especially likes children."

"We're not children," said Benny.

"Well, no," agreed Grandfather. "But George April would think you were. Wait until you see the things he has in April Center."

"What things?" asked Benny.

"Now don't rush me," said Mr. Alden. "A few years ago, George April bought some land and built April Center. It is a small place in the country, but very famous. I had no idea it was so near. People come here from all over the United States. No cars are allowed. You have to leave your car at the gate. After you pay to enter, you can walk around April

Center. Or you can hire a horse and driver by the hour. The drivers wait at the gate."

Benny opened his mouth to speak and then shut it again. Grandfather noticed.

"Good, Ben," he said. "You know I am telling this as fast as I can. There is a village green in the middle of April Center—a park with green grass and trees. George sent me a picture postcard of the place once. A road goes right around the edge of the green. There are a lot of buildings all along the street—all different. I remember there's an old country store. There's also a doll museum and an animal museum. In the animal museum you can see mounted wild animals and even stones with dinosaur tracks."

"I'd love to see the dolls," said Violet. "They must be interesting."

"I'm sure they are," said Mr. Alden. "I've never seen the place myself. But I'd like to."

"So would I," said Henry. "I'll pole the boat up to the dock."

The Aldens soon stepped ashore, and Henry dropped the anchor. Both doors of the houseboat were locked and the windows shut. Benny tied the rope. He said, "We will never forget to lock this houseboat. We don't want to come back again and find that a stranger has been here."

They started down the path, but they did not walk far before they saw the gate.

Many people were visiting April Center that day. As the Aldens paid for their tickets, they saw parents walking along with their children. On the other side of the gate they could see the village green.

Inside the gate, a horse hitched to a strange-looking wagon was standing under a tree. A small, thin man in a red coat was the driver. The Aldens looked once at the man, but they looked twice at the horse.

"What a thin horse!" said Benny. "I can see his ribs."

Mr. Alden said, "I don't understand this. That horse isn't well fed. George wouldn't have such a thin horse on his place. I'm sure he doesn't know about this."

The driver saw the Aldens. He climbed down from his old wagon. He took off his cap. "See the Center, sir?" he asked Mr. Alden with a bow. "My name's Sam. Dolly and I go right around the Center.

We'll wait at every building as long as you want."

Benny looked at Sam and said, "You can't take five of us. We're too heavy. That horse can't pull us all."

"Oh, yes she can," said Sam. "Dolly, you're used to it, aren't you, girl?" Sam patted Dolly gently. "See, she doesn't mind at all. This carriage holds six."

Indeed, there were three seats, and each seat had room for two persons. Without another word, Benny climbed into the front seat beside the driver. Grandfather and Violet sat behind them, and Jessie and Henry took the back seat. Dolly started down the street.

"Go along, pet," said Sam. "Go along, old girl. You like hot weather. You know you do."

Benny looked up at Sam. "You don't come from around here, do you?" he asked.

"No. I'm an old jockey. I'm so small I used to be a jockey in the Blue Grass Country. But I've been up here for five years. Now, ladies," said Sam, looking over his shoulder, "over there is the country store. Then come some old-fashioned houses. And next is the doll museum."

"Let's go to the doll museum first," said Jessie. "We can't see every building in one day."

"No," said Sam. "It takes two days. Some people stay a week."

Benny said suddenly, "Tell me, Sam, why is Dolly so thin?"

Sam shook his gray head. "I know she's too thin. It makes me feel poorly. Maybe Dolly's just a thin horse. I feed her as well as I can."

Mr. Alden said, "Sam, doesn't Mr. April pay you well? He's a good friend of mine."

Sam sat up very straight. "Oh, yes, sir! Mr. April pays me fine. He's a good man. Don't ever say anything bad about Mr. April! He can't come here very often. He lives in London."

"Yes, he does," said Grandfather. "But he wouldn't like to see such a thin horse on his place."

But Sam only said, "Giddap, old girl. Stop at the doll museum."

Dolly began to trot. She stopped in front of the museum.

"We'll wait right here," said Sam. "Take your time. Stay as long as you like."

The Aldens went up the front walk. Mr. Alden said, "Something is wrong here. I'd like to know what it is."

Violet said, "Sam loves his horse. You can see that. Did you notice that Dolly was brushed till she shone like silk?"

"Yes," said Mr. Alden. "That's why it's so strange. Sam takes good care of Dolly, but neither one gets enough to eat."

Henry laughed just a little. He said, "Grandfather, you know most people wouldn't even notice a thin horse. And they wouldn't care if they did."

"Yes, Henry, I know. But this family loves animals, and we can't help noticing them."

The Aldens had reached the door. "Well, here are

the dolls," Grandfather said.

"What a wonderful place!" said Violet when they walked inside. Even Henry and Benny were fascinated. A young girl in an old-fashioned costume came to meet them.

"Let me show you this dollhouse," she said. "Notice the man doll sitting in that easy chair? He is six inches tall. He is reading a newspaper that is just the size of a postage stamp. You can see it is printed exactly like a big one. Now let me show you his set of checkers."

The girl picked up a tiny black box from the little doll table. It was so small that she could hardly hold it. She opened it. The box and cover made a tiny checkerboard, and twenty-four red and black checkers were inside.

"This game is even smaller than a postage stamp," said the girl.

Violet said, "I don't see how anyone made those checkers so small."

"This dollhouse is one hundred years old," said the girl.

"Look at that beautiful doll's tea set!" said Jessie,

pointing to another tiny room in the dollhouse.

"Yes, some people think that is the smallest china tea set in the world," said the girl. "The little handles are real gold, and the roses are painted by hand."

"We'd better not touch that," said Violet.

Benny was looking around the room. Suddenly he said, "Look over there!" He pointed to a corner where many people were standing. The Aldens walked across the room.

On a large wooden table was a model of a Pennsylvania farm. Everything in the model was carved and painted by hand.

A wooden man was sitting on a milking stool beside a cow. Hens and chickens stood around the barnyard. A woman doll stood among them with a tiny basket of corn. Two horses were hitched to a wagon with a black top. A boy doll stood beside a well, with his hand on the pump handle.

The girl said to Benny, "Just turn that switch." Benny did so.

Suddenly the farm came to life with a great rattle. The man began to milk the cow. The woman began to throw the corn. The hens began to peck the corn.

The boy began to pump the well. Real water ran out of the pump into a pail. The two horses began to trot down the road.

What a great noise—clack, clack! Everyone watching the model began to laugh. A woman standing near the Aldens said, "That is the cleverest thing I ever saw in my life!"

At last Jessie said, "Grandfather, we'll never have time to see all these things. Maybe we ought to go into another building that Benny likes."

"Yes, my dear. What do you want to see, Benny?" Grandfather asked.

"The animals," said Benny.

The Aldens went out, looking at more dolls on the way. Sam and Dolly were waiting outside, but both of them seemed to be asleep. Just then another horse and carriage exactly like Sam's came trotting along with a load of people.

"That horse is as thin as Dolly," said Henry in surprise. "And the man looks like Sam, doesn't he?"

"Maybe he is Sam's brother," said Benny. "Maybe the horse is Dolly's sister."

Grandfather laughed. He didn't know then that

Benny was exactly right.

The Aldens didn't want to wake Sam and Dolly so they went on foot down the street. Soon they came to a bright red brick building. Over the door was the word "Animals." The Aldens went inside.

In this building they saw beautifully-mounted foxes and wolves, a deer, and a raccoon. But Benny went straight for a small dinosaur standing in the middle of the room. It was about as tall as Benny, but the sign said, "This is a model of a dinosaur fifteen feet tall and forty feet long."

"Just think!" said Jessie, looking at the model. "Those animals used to be walking around here."

Benny said, "If one of them stepped on me, he wouldn't even know it."

"That's right, Ben," said Henry. "Just the way we step on a bug and don't know it."

Along the sides of the room were large stones with dinosaur footprints in them. One footprint looked like a bird's and another like an elephant's. There were dinosaurs' leg bones that were taller than Benny.

Soon Jessie said, "I must think about cooking supper. I think we ought to go, Henry. But I'm sure we want to come again tomorrow. We can sleep in the houseboat right at the dock."

Benny said, "We *must* come back tomorrow. We have to find out more about Sam."

Sam and Dolly were still asleep when the Aldens came out of the museum. But the second horse was going by with a load of people. Henry happened to look at his grandfather. Mr. Alden was staring at the second horse. He looked from one horse to the other.

"Henry!" said Grandfather. "Those two horses are a matched pair! I'm sure they came from the Blue Grass country. If I'm right, they were once beautiful horses, worth a great deal of money."

Benny looked at Sam, fast asleep. Then he looked at the other driver. He exclaimed, "You can hardly tell those two drivers apart! One's awake and one's asleep. That's the only difference."

Jessie said, "You're right, Ben. They look like twins."

Benny said, "A matched pair of horses and a matched pair of drivers!"

"Shh, Ben. They'll hear you," said Jessie.

Indeed, someone at April Center did hear Benny. A

workman said, "That is a matched pair of horses, all right. I can remember when they first came here. They held their heads up high. The old jockeys did, too."

"What's the matter with the horses now?" asked Benny.

The man shrugged his shoulders. "Don't ask me," he said, walking away.

Benny called after the man, "Are the two men brothers?"

"Yes," answered the man. "Sam and Jeff. The horses are Dolly and Molly."

The Aldens walked to the dock without waking Sam. It seemed strange to eat supper on the houseboat when it was quietly resting at the dock.

"Well, we learned a little about Sam," said Benny. "His brother's name is Jeff. I'm glad we're spending another day at April Center. I want to see the country store tomorrow. And besides, I have a plan in mind."

Violet smiled. "I suppose you don't want to tell us your plan?"

"No," said Benny. "Not yet."

CHAPTER 6

Something Wrong

The next morning the Aldens waited only long enough to eat breakfast and change the name of the houseboat.

Benny climbed up the ladder to change the letters. He said, "I hate to take *The Watch Alden* down. But you've had your day, Watch. Today it will be *The Mrs. McGregor*."

When Benny climbed down, Henry was saying, "I wish we could find out why those horses are so thin. We know that Mr. April pays Sam well."

Jessie added, "Sam said he gives as much as he can to Dolly."

"And we know Sam loves his horse," said Violet. "It doesn't seem to make sense."

Benny thought a minute. Then he laughed. "The only way to find out is to ask Sam," he said.

"Oh, no," said Jessie, shaking her head. "I would never ask Sam!"

"I would," said Benny. "I bet Sam would tell me."

Henry laughed. "I bet he would, too, Ben. Try it! No harm done if he won't tell."

Violet said, "Sam likes Benny. I think he would say that Benny was comical, just as Mr. Rivers did."

So the Aldens locked up the houseboat and went back to April Center. As they walked through the gate Benny looked around for Sam. But Sam was nowhere in sight.

"You'll like the country store, Ben," said Henry, walking along. "They will have everything in there—cloth, sugar, cheese, and a cracker barrel."

The cracker barrel was the first thing the Aldens saw when they went into the store. The storekeeper looked up at Benny and said, "Help yourself to a cracker!"

There was a hole in the cover of the wooden barrel. Benny put his hand into the hole and pulled out a cracker. Henry came next. He said to the man, "That hole is almost too small for my hand."

"That is why the hole was made small," replied the man. "Nobody can get two crackers out at one time. They used to try in the old days, but they never could do it."

Three old men were sitting around an old stove, smoking pipes. Grandfather looked around the room and said, "This looks exactly like the old country store I went in when I was a boy. See the old-fashioned stick candy?"

"Red-and-white stripes," said Benny. "I bet it is peppermint."

The storekeeper said, "Try the coffee grinder, folks. Right over there."

They all went to look at the coffee grinder. Jessie said, "I don't suppose you sell the coffee, do you?"

"Oh, yes, I do," the storekeeper answered. "You can buy coffee, candy, cheese, and oats for horses. All the other things are just to look at."

Jessie said, "We'll take a pound of coffee, then."

The man poured a pound of brown coffee beans into the coffee mill. He said to Benny, "Grind away, son!"

Benny took the handle and turned it round and round. It was hard work. The ground coffee came out in a bag and was all ready to use.

"Did you say you sell cheese?" asked Mr. Alden.

"Right here!" The man showed them an enormous round cheese, as big as an automobile tire. "I'll cut off whatever you want."

"I never saw such a big cheese," said Jessie. "I'll take a pound."

"Now what about oats for a horse?" asked Henry.

"Yes, we sell oats," said the man. "But what do you want oats for?"

"I was thinking about Sam's horse, Dolly," said Henry.

The storeman stopped smiling and shook his head. "It's a funny thing about that," he said. "Sam used to buy a lot of oats for Dolly. And his brother Jeff did, too. But they don't buy so much now. Not half as much as they used to. I can't understand it. It's been going on for almost a year."

Benny said, "Oh, let's buy some oats for Sam. We can tell him it's a birthday present for Dolly."

Henry nodded. The man took a big bag of oats out

OLD TIME
GOO

of a corner and gave it to Henry.

As the Aldens went out to the street, they saw Sam and Dolly. Sam had no customers, but he smiled at the Aldens.

Benny said to his family, "You go along. I'd rather stay here with Sam. He isn't busy right now. I'll be along soon."

Benny climbed up into the wagon and sat down beside the old jockey.

"How is Dolly today?" he asked.

"Fine," said Sam. "See her ears now? She knows we're talking about her." Indeed, her ears were turned backwards.

"I've been thinking, Sam," said Benny. "It seems to me that you are in some kind of trouble."

The old driver turned to the young boy and said, "That is surely kind of you. Most people don't care about an old carriage-driver."

"I care," said Benny.

"I know you do," said Sam.

"Well, Sam, *are* you in trouble?"

"No, not exactly," said Sam.

"What do you mean, *not exactly?*" asked Benny.

"Well, I got no trouble myself, but I hear that my brother Jeff has. So I feel poorly. Yes, boy, I'm sure enough worried about Jeff."

The man and the boy sat a while without saying a word.

Then Benny said, "Sam, my grandfather is a smart man. Maybe he could get Jeff out of trouble."

"No, boy. Nobody could do that," Sam answered.

Benny put his hand on Sam's arm. "Now, Sam! What a silly thing to say! You don't know what my family can do when we get started. But how can we help you when we don't know what the trouble is? Don't you trust me?"

Sam drew a long breath. "I'd like to trust you, boy. I'd surely like to!"

"Well, then, tell me about Jeff. Has he done anything wrong?"

Sam turned and looked at Benny. "I know Jeff wouldn't do anything wrong. I don't believe it! I never believed it!"

"Who says he's done something wrong?" asked Benny.

"Well, somebody says he has," answered Sam.

"But I can't tell you who it is. Then I'd be in trouble."

"You're in trouble now," said Benny.

Sam was thinking. He looked at Benny for a long time. He knew he could trust Benny. Sam took a deep breath and said, "I'm going to tell you, boy. A man comes to me every month and I give him half my pay. If I don't, he says he will tell the police about Jeff."

"I see," said Benny, nodding his head. "So that is why you can't afford to feed Dolly enough."

"Yes, that's why. I give Dolly as much as I can. But I have to eat, too."

Benny nodded again. Then he said, "Would you believe me, Sam, if I said you would be out of trouble soon?"

"I don't know," said Sam. "That would be a great day."

Benny began to climb out of the wagon. He said, "Well, don't worry anymore, Sam. It won't be long now!"

Benny walked away. As he looked back, he saw three people getting into Sam's wagon. He stepped out of sight. He waited until Sam had turned the wagon around and trotted off. Then Benny walked slowly down the street looking for Jeff. He found him outside an old-fashioned house waiting for his customers.

Benny looked up at Jeff and said, "May I come and sit with you a minute?"

"Sure," said Jeff. He was surprised.

When Benny was in the front seat, he said, "You don't know me, Jeff, but Sam does."

"Yes, I know you," said Jeff. "Sam told me all about the Aldens. He said the old man is very kind."

"You mean my grandfather?" asked Benny. "He isn't old."

"Oh, I don't mean old," said Jeff. "He's just grown up."

"I wonder if you would talk to me, Jeff," asked Benny.

"Oh, yes, I'd like to talk to you. Any of your family. I'd be glad to."

"Well, then," said Benny, "tell me this. Are you in trouble?"

Jeff turned around to Benny just as his brother had done. "No," he said. "But don't tell Sam."

"Why?" asked Benny. "I won't tell Sam."

"I just worry about Sam," said Jeff. "I hear tell *he* is in trouble. So I worry all the time."

Benny said, "Do you think Sam has done anything wrong?"

"No!" said Jeff. "Sam wouldn't. He's my twin brother."

"But somebody told you he has. Is that right?" asked Benny.

"Yes, that's right. But I still don't believe him. And don't you tell, boy!"

"I won't," said Benny. "You know, Jeff, I thought something was wrong."

"Now why did you ever think that?" asked Jeff.

"Well, because Molly is so thin," said Benny.

"Think of that!" said Jeff. "Nobody cares about an old thin horse."

"*You* care a lot about Molly, don't you?" asked Benny.

"Oh, yes. I brush her and brush her. See how she shines?"

"But you don't feed her very well," said Benny quietly.

"No," said Jeff sadly. "But I do the best I can."

"I know that," said Benny. He began to climb down. He had learned what he wanted to know. Then he had an idea. He said, "By the way, Jeff, have you seen two men in a big black car driving around April Center? I'm interested in cars and it's a special one."

Jeff looked quickly at Benny and then away. It seemed as if he was going to nod, but he said, "Two men in a black car? I see lots of men and lots of black cars. They all look alike to me."

Jeff looked so worried that Benny said, "Jeff, don't worry anymore. In four or five days everything will be all right."

"What do you mean, boy?" asked Jeff.

"I can't tell you that because I don't know what it will be myself. But you'll see very soon."

"Don't you tell Sam!" Jeff warned.

"No, I won't," promised Benny. He almost ran to find his family. He felt light as a feather! How wonderful it would be when Sam and Jeff were happy again, and Molly and Dolly had enough to eat. He was sure Henry and Jessie could think of some way to help the old jockeys.

Benny found his family just leaving an old house. Jessie saw Benny coming.

"Oh, let's go home," she said. "We can hear all about Sam and Dolly on the boat where nobody is listening."

"Let's give this heavy bag of oats to Sam first," said Henry.

Jeff came by just then with an empty wagon. He heard what Henry said. "I'll see that Sam gets it," he said, stopping his horse.

"Good," said Henry. "Please take some oats for Molly, too." Henry lifted the bag into Jeff's front seat. "Thank you," said Henry. "That will save time."

"Thank *you*," said Jeff, driving off.

The houseboat, *The Mrs. McGregor*, was just as they had left it. Henry poled it out into the river, and the Alden family sat down on the deck to talk. Benny told his story to the end.

Then Henry said, "You did well, Ben. We know now what is bothering Sam and Jeff. Let's think of everything else that seems wrong. First, that vase was lost at the auction. And Mrs. Young and her sister are worried, too."

Jessie said, "Don't forget the waitress in the restaurant."

"Yes, the waitress," agreed Henry. "Then the smoke on this boat. Oh, by the way, Ben. A policeman came into the old house while we were there, and I told him about our clock. He said he would tell Mr. Rivers."

"Good!" said Benny.

"We still don't know why the boy in the red cap ran away from the auction so fast," said Violet.

"And remember, the two policemen said something strange was going on up and down this river," said Mr. Alden.

Benny said, "And the black car!"

"Right. The black car and the two men," said Jessie. "Do you think the black car has anything to do with all these people, Henry?"

Henry replied, "Yes, that is exactly what I do think."

Benny added, "But remember, we've still got four or five days!"

CHAPTER 7

Mystery in a Picture

The next day at breakfast Benny said, "Let's name the houseboat *The Sam and Dolly* today. That would make Sam laugh if he could see it."

The family always ate on the deck now. They liked it better than the galley.

Benny looked at the row of gulls sitting on the railing. "The only trouble with eating out here is you gulls," he said. "You watch every bite."

Jessie said, "I wonder where all those gulls go. They just come here for meals."

Mr. Alden replied, "They must go fifty miles down the river to the ocean."

When breakfast was over, the gulls flew away. Benny climbed up the ladder to change the name of the houseboat. It was *The Sam and Dolly* today.

Violet was holding a glass of orange juice in her hand. She stood up to watch Benny and stepped back to see better. Her foot hit the sandbox. Splash! Orange juice went everywhere. It was all over the clean white sand.

"Oh, look where it went!" said Violet. "We need that sand to put out fires. Wait! I can get it off." She took a spoon and a cup. Then she very carefully scraped off every bit of wet sand.

"I don't think I lost a spoonful of sand," she said.

"No harm done," said Jessie. "We promised to keep the sandbox filled up to the line and it is."

The Aldens floated slowly down the beautiful river. They sat on the front deck.

Benny was looking straight down the river from the roof. He said, "Something is right in the way. What is it?"

Henry said, "It looks like an island."

It was indeed an island, but a very small one. Here the river was a little wider. As the Aldens floated nearer, they saw that the island was made of rock. A few bushes grew here and there on small spots of sand. As they came still nearer, a great crowd of sea gulls rose in the air, calling and screaming.

Benny climbed down the ladder. "This is where the gulls live!" he said. "There must be a million."

Henry laughed. He said, "Hold on, Ben. Not a million, but a lot of gulls for one small island."

There were some posts in the water. Henry said, "This was once a dock. You can see where it was. Let's float in. We've already scared the gulls anyway."

The gulls had flown off, but when the boat stopped moving, the birds began to come back. One by one they came. Some sat on the posts. Some landed on the rocks. The place was soon thick with gulls.

"Let's call this Gull Island," Benny said.

Henry pointed at an enormous gull on a post. "What a picture that would make!" he said. He rushed to the cabin to get his camera.

"Take two pictures," said Jessie. "One may not come out very well. Oh, look at the duck!" She pointed at a bird which was flying back again behind the rocks. "Let's go ashore and see where it went."

The Aldens stepped into the water from the boat

and waded ashore. The gulls rose in the air, screaming loudly. The Aldens climbed over the stones and looked over the top of the big rock. There was the duck swimming around in the water. Seven baby ducks followed her. Sometimes they put their bills in the water and caught bugs. Sometimes they turned upside down.

Violet said, "Aren't they cute, Henry? See if you can get a picture of a duckling upside down. You can only see its tail."

Henry snapped the camera. He said, "I think two of them were upside down, and the mother duck, too."

Something made Benny look away from the island toward the riverbank. There stood a lovely white bird!

"Look, Henry!" Benny whispered. "Take a picture. It's a white heron."

Benny waded back to the boat and asked Grandfather for the field glasses. He looked through them at the bird. It was beautiful, standing on one leg in the water, its lacy white topknot blowing in the wind.

"That's an egret," said Grandfather. "Sometimes

they fly this far north. Take its picture, Henry."

The bird was quiet, and Henry could work slowly. He snapped one picture and then another.

Benny looked through the field glasses again. All at once he whispered, "Henry! Something is behind that egret. Something white. Just look."

Henry looked in the camera finder. Then he looked toward the bird as if he were going to take another picture.

Benny whispered, "I think it's a man in a white shirt."

"Right, Ben," agreed Henry. "But why is he hiding behind a tree? He thinks the tree hides him, but I can see an arm sticking out on each side."

Snap, went the camera. "I have a picture of two arms and two shoulders," said Henry. "I wonder if he came here to watch us? And why?"

"I don't know," said Benny. "But I think that is just what he's doing." Then one arm moved.

"Keep watching him," said Benny excitedly. "If he starts to leave, take another picture."

A minute went by. Suddenly the man moved. He didn't walk or run. He bent down and scrambled through the bushes. Henry snapped two more pictures before the man was out of sight.

"I hope these pictures are good," Benny said.

Grandfather said, "It's too bad Henry doesn't have his long-distance lens on the camera."

"I do," said Henry. "All these pictures will be big. And now the next thing is to get these pictures printed."

"Right," said Benny. "Let's watch for a landing."

The four Aldens climbed aboard the houseboat, and Henry poled it away from the island. Soon they were floating down the river.

Benny and Henry watched the riverbanks for a landing. Benny was looking for something else, too. He thought he might see the man in the white shirt again, but he did not. Once he thought he saw a car parked in the woods, but he wasn't sure. It was not far from Gull Island.

At last *The Sam and Dolly* came to a landing. Even in their excitement the Aldens did not forget to lock the houseboat.

When they found a drugstore in the small town, Benny spoke to the clerk. He said, "We have some very important pictures in our camera. How soon can we have prints?"

The clerk laughed. He said, "I'm sure you must have pictures of the President of the United States. I do develop my own pictures. I'm not very busy so I'll develop the film right now if you hand it over."

"Oh, thank you!" said five voices. "We'll wait."

The clerk began to think the pictures were really important. "You can sit at the counter," he said. "I'll hurry."

In less than half an hour the man handed Henry prints of the pictures. The Aldens crowded around and Violet said, "Those pictures are large. That lens is a wonderful thing, Henry."

Then Benny said one single word, "Look!"

He pointed at the white shoulders of the man in the bushes. Right behind him was a very faint picture of a face!

"There were *two* men," said Benny.

Henry studied the picture. "There certainly is another man," he agreed.

Violet said, "Do you think the men were watching our houseboat? They must have some reason for hiding from us. What could it be?"

"Benny and I think the men were watching us, too," Henry said. "They wouldn't hide if they weren't doing something wrong."

"Do you think we ought to give these pictures to the police?" asked Benny.

"Yes," said Grandfather. "But let's go back to the houseboat first."

"Yes," said Henry. "I have a feeling somebody wants to get on the houseboat when we are not there. It happened once. It could happen again."

Henry and Benny soon poled the boat away from the landing. Once again they were in the middle of the river.

Henry put the pictures in his suitcase.

"A boat is coming!" called Jessie.

"I see it," said Grandfather. "It's the Coast Guard. Maybe they have heard of a houseboat with too many names and want to look us over. The Coast Guard has to do that. It has to find out what every boat is doing. And if any boatman is breaking the law, the Coast Guard can go aboard and search the boat. It can even arrest a boatman."

Two men were on the Coast Guard boat. They steered carefully around *The Sam and Dolly.*

The men shouted to Henry, "Want to drop your anchor?" Henry threw it overboard at once.

"Come aboard," called Grandfather. "My name is James Alden."

"Yes, I know," said the older man, smiling. He had several large fish on a string. He stepped aboard the houseboat, but the other man stayed on the Coast Guard boat.

"We just pulled these fellows out of the river. Would you like them?"

Jessie smiled and took the fish with thanks.

The stranger went on, "The houseboat has so many names that I wanted to see the crew."

"Well, these are my grandchildren," said Mr. Alden. "This is Captain Henry and his first mate, Benny. Jessie is the cook, and Violet the washer-woman."

"I'm Commander Williams," said the man. "I hope the washerwoman is stronger than she looks."

"Yes, Violet is a tough girl," said Benny. "Come and see our laundry tub. Come right through the cabin to the rear deck and I'll show you."

The Commander went along with Benny. He noticed that everything was clean. He even noticed the fire pail and the sandbox. But before he had time to look for a laundry tub, Violet had jumped into the river and was climbing into the rope seat.

"Well, I never saw anything like that!" exclaimed Commander Williams. "Did you make it?"

"Henry made it," said Violet. "I do the washing, and Jessie hangs it out." Then she swam off and climbed up on the deck.

"Your boat is all shipshape," the commander said. "You do very well with your housekeeping. Do you enjoy this kind of life?"

"Oh, we're having a neat time!" answered Benny. "Something new every day."

"Is that so?" said the visitor. "What, for instance?"

Suddenly the Aldens looked serious and Mr. Alden said, "I'm really very glad you came, Commander."

"We all feel that something is wrong," said Henry.

"Wrong with the houseboat?"

"The houseboat is all right. The trouble is along the river," said Henry.

Benny said, "We're beginning to think there is something mysterious going on."

"Well, I must tell you that the police officers think this, too," said Mr. Williams. "They asked the Coast Guard to help. We often work together. They think something is going on, but they need some proof."

"We may have some proof," said Henry. "Let me show you the pictures I took at Gull Island." He got the pictures of the white egret and handed them to the commander.

"Very good!" said Mr. Williams. He took out a small magnifying glass to look at the pictures.

"Do you see what I see, Captain Henry?" he asked.

"Well, I see the man hiding and the face of another man farther away, if that's what you mean."

"No, I mean the black ring on the man's left hand." He handed the glass and the best picture to Henry.

Henry looked closely through the glass. "Well, we missed it!" he said. "I never noticed that ring. Did you, Jessie?"

"No," said Jessie. "Let me look."

"Me, too," said Benny.

Benny looked at the picture. "Oh!" he said excitedly. "I've seen that black ring before, Henry! Don't you remember at the Elm Tree Inn I told you about the man who drove so fast with his right hand? That very ring was on his left hand. I saw it as he held the window!"

"Yes," said Henry. "I remember."

The commander said, "Good! Then that's one more thing we know." He leaned back in his chair. "What else do you know about this trouble along the river?" He looked at Benny as he spoke.

"We know six people who are worried. They are all too scared to talk. Then somebody took a vase at the auction at Pomfret Landing."

Jessie said, "When we came back to the houseboat after the auction, we smelled cigarette smoke. Our clock was gone. We think someone has a key."

Commander Williams nodded. He said, "Maybe I can explain that. Before you came, there was a family who named the houseboat *The Blue Heron.* They were careless with the key. One day they left it in the lock all morning while they went shopping. I happened to need a new key for my supply room, so I went to the locksmith. I was surprised to see a man slipping out the back way. I asked the locksmith who it was, but he didn't want to tell. That made me wonder. At last he said that the man had wanted a new key to match the one from Mr. Rivers' houseboat. So maybe that is how someone got in while you were away."

"But who was the man?" asked Benny.

"That's what I don't know," said the commander. "Maybe it would help if you'd tell me the names of the people who are worried."

"Sam and Jeff at April Center," began Benny. "And Mrs. Young and her sister at the candy store at Pomfret Landing, and a waitress at Second Landing. And I don't know about a boy in a red cap."

"You don't think the boy in the red cap was the person on your houseboat while you were gone?"

"No!" said Benny. "I don't think he was. I liked him."

"Do you know that the boy in the red cap is Mrs. Young's son?"

"No," answered Benny. "So that's why she is so worried!"

"Yes, she has plenty to worry about. That boy came home with twenty-five dollars and wouldn't tell his mother where he got it. She thinks he is getting into trouble."

"I think she's right," nodded Henry.

Commander Williams stood up. "Now I must go. If you let me have one of those pictures, I'll pass it on to the police. It may help them."

"Glad to help," said Henry.

"Thank you for the fish," added Jessie.

CHAPTER 8

A Discovery

Jessie called, "Lunch! We have a surprise for you, Benny."

Benny took one look at his plate. On it was a piece of Commander Williams' fish and a pile of fluffy mashed potatoes.

"Oh, mashed potatoes!" shouted Benny. "You're a nice sister, Jessie! But where did you get them?"

"Out of a box," said Jessie. "It's instant potato."

Halfway through lunch Henry looked out over the river and began to laugh. "We're still at anchor," he said. "I forgot to pull up the anchor after Commander Williams left."

"I guess we're going nowhere in a hurry," said Benny.

When everything was eaten, Jessie said, "If you all help, we'll be through our work in a hurry. Henry, will you take these fish heads and tails and throw them to the gulls? They must have known we had fish."

It happened that Henry had the houseboat key in his hand when Jessie called him. He picked up the scraps and went to the back deck. He raised his arm as high as he could and threw—not the fish heads—but the door key!

"Jessie!" Henry yelled. "Dive with me! Swim right where I swim!"

Jessie did not know what it was all about, but she did exactly what Henry told her. She dived in and followed him.

Henry gasped, "I threw the door key! I haven't taken my eyes off the spot. I know just where it went."

"We'll dive for it," said Jessie, swimming faster.

"Here!" said Henry. He put his head down and disappeared. Jessie followed.

In a minute they both came up. "I saw it!" gasped Jessie, "but I couldn't stay down."

"Same here," sputtered Henry. They both went down again. By this time the family was watching from the rear deck.

"Stay here, Benny," Grandfather said. "You'll just stir up the water so they can't see. Two is enough. Ha! Good for you, Henry!"

Henry came up, holding the key. Jessie came up. They swam quickly to the boat and climbed aboard.

Henry made a bow to Jessie and gave her the key. "Put it around your neck on a chain," he said. "I'm not fit to carry a key!"

"Oh, yes, you are," said Grandfather. "You did very well to see exactly where the key went."

Then Benny said, "But look where all the fish heads and scraps went—all over the sandbox!"

Benny held up a fish tail and called. The air was full of gulls in an instant. They caught all the scraps before they landed in the water.

Jessie sniffed. "That sand will always smell fishy. We can't have that on a boat. We'll have to get some new sand."

Benny began to laugh. He said, "Henry, you ought to have seen yourself! Throwing that key as far as you could and dropping the fish bones. That was pretty neat!"

Violet pointed toward the shore. "Isn't that a nice white beach?" she asked. "We can empty the box and fill it up with clean sand."

"It looks fine," said Mr. Alden. "Let's pole the boat

in, Henry."

"I'll go and empty the sandbox," said Benny. "We can just dump the sand in the water."

"I'll help you," said Jessie. "Sand is heavy."

The two dragged the sandbox to the rear deck and tipped it over. The sand poured smoothly into the river.

"The sand looks like water," said Benny. "It's like a waterfall."

But suddenly, what was this flashing thing in the bottom of the box, under the sand? Before Jessie or Benny could do anything it went into the river, with a flash of red and green and gold.

"The vase—the vase from the auction!" Benny shouted. In an instant he dived into the water. Jessie followed him, shouting "Henry!"

Henry heard his name and came running. Mr. Alden and Violet came, too. Just then Benny came up gasping. "It's the vase on the desk!" he said.

Jessie came up, gasping. "I see it! It is that vase. You try, Henry."

Down went Henry. In no time he was up again with the vase in his hand.

"Terrific!" yelled Benny.

"Good thing," said Henry as he tried to get his breath, "the boat is hardly moving. The vase was right there on top of the white sand."

Jessie, Benny, and Henry climbed on board, breathing hard. They looked at the vase.

Violet said, "It is just what the auctioneer said, gold with rubies and emeralds."

"But how did it get in our sandbox?" asked Jessie.

"I know!" said Benny. "The one who came aboard our houseboat thought it was a safe hiding place. I'm sure!"

Mr. Alden said, "I'm sure, too."

Benny said, "I'll tell you what. Let's go and get that clean sand. We might still have a fire on board and need sand to put it out. When the sandbox is filled, Henry can start the motor and we'll go back to the auction place."

Henry nodded. "That's good, Ben. I certainly want to put this vase in a safe place. And we know there is a policeman at that landing."

Henry and Benny poled the boat to the sandy beach. Henry jumped out with the empty box and waded ashore. He filled the box up to the line and came back with it on his shoulder.

Mr. Alden reached down and took the box. Henry climbed back on the boat. "This is the day when we are in and out of the water," he said.

Henry and Mr. Alden turned the houseboat around to head up the river. Henry started the motor in the rear. Off they went! How strange it seemed to be going so fast.

Past Gull Island, past their old landings, past the red-winged blackbirds, past April Center. At last Violet said, "I see the auction sign ahead."

Henry turned off the motor and poled the boat up to the landing. The Aldens walked up the path, Benny carrying the vase in the empty mashed-potato box.

"Who'd ever guess what we have?" Benny asked. "A potato box is just the thing for a treasure."

CHAPTER 9

The Plan

When the Aldens came to the auction building they found the door open. But nobody was inside.

"No auction today," said Benny. "This isn't Saturday."

"Well, let's look for someone to help us," Jessie said. So the Aldens walked slowly down the main street, looking for a policeman. There were not many people on the street because there was no auction.

"There's the Elm Tree Inn," Violet said, pointing.

Benny exclaimed, "Quick! The boy with the red cap! He's going into the Elm Tree Inn."

"No, Ben," said Jessie. "That boy hasn't any cap at all. And besides he didn't look like that boy to me."

"He did to me," said Benny. "Let's go in and see."

The Aldens went in. Nobody was in the dining room. But Benny and Violet saw a boy go through a door in the back.

"Hey, wait a minute!" called Benny. "Just one minute, please!"

The boy half turned and stood still.

Henry said, "It's all right. Don't be afraid. You're Mrs. Young's boy, aren't you?"

The boy looked up. "What of it? What do you want?"

"We're trying to find a policeman," Jessie said.

"I can't help you," the boy said.

"Aren't you the boy who bought the clothes at the auction?" Benny asked. "We were there, too."

The boy did not say anything.

"Why did you want the clothes?" Violet asked. "Did you need them?"

"Those old clothes?" the boy said suddenly. "We're not that poor. A man asked me to buy them for him. He said he was too busy to go to an auction himself."

"Did he give you money to do that?" Benny asked.

"Maybe twenty-five dollars?" asked Henry.

The boy looked at the Aldens. He decided he could trust them. "Yes, that's right. I didn't do anything wrong. I just bought the box and gave it to the man. What's wrong with that?"

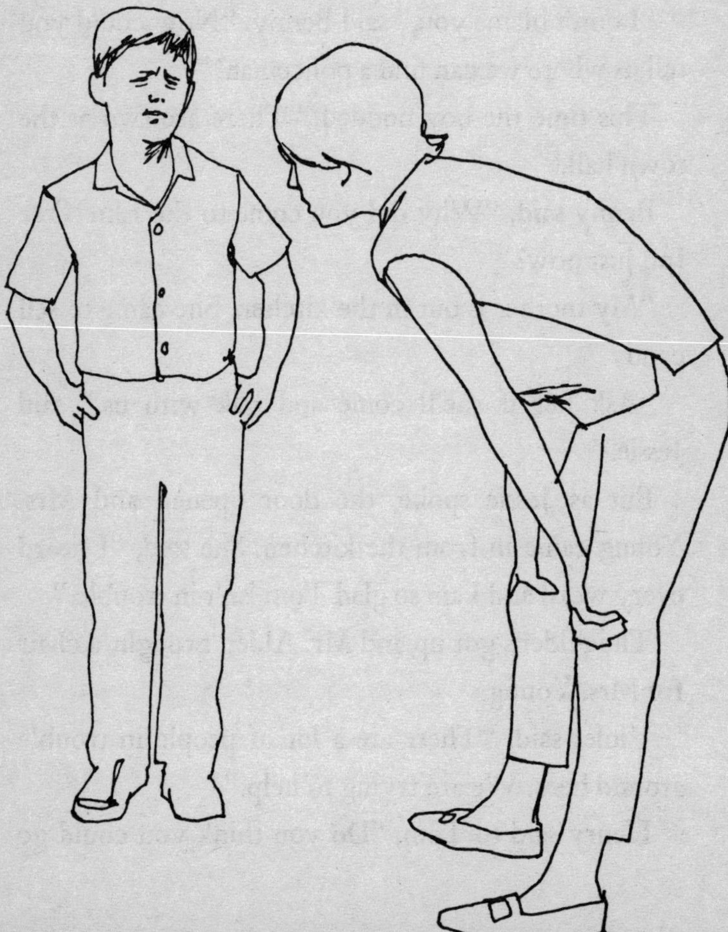

"Nothing," replied Benny. "Have you ever seen the man again?"

"Yes," the boy said. "I saw him today at the Princess Hotel. He was talking to another man. I ran before he saw me. I don't like him."

"I don't blame you," said Benny. "Now could you tell us where we can find a policeman?"

This time the boy nodded. "There are two at the town hall."

Benny said, "Why did you come to the Elm Tree Inn just now?"

"My mother is out in the kitchen. She came to sell candy."

"Ask her if she'll come and talk with us," said Jessie.

But as Jessie spoke, the door opened and Mrs. Young came in from the kitchen. She said, "I heard every word and I am so glad Tom isn't in trouble."

The Aldens got up and Mr. Alden brought a chair for Mrs. Young.

Violet said, "There are a lot of people in trouble around here. We are trying to help."

Henry said to Tom, "Do you think you could go

out the back door and get one of those policemen to come in the back way?"

"Easy!" said Tom Young. "I'll tell him it's the folks from the houseboat." Then he was gone.

"He knew us all the time!" said Benny.

"Everybody knows you," said Mrs. Young. "These towns up and down the river are quite small. You will find that almost everyone knows your names and when you stop for the night."

Just then a few people went by, looking in the window.

Mr. Alden said quickly, "Before that policeman comes, do you suppose we could go into the kitchen? People can see us too well from here."

"Oh, yes," replied Mrs. Young. "The lady who runs this inn won't mind. She will let you sit in the small dining room through that door."

In a few minutes Tom came in with a policeman.

"Sit down," said Mr. Alden. "We are all glad to see you. Look!" He pointed at Benny.

The policeman looked at Benny, who began to open the mashed-potato box. He put in his hand and pulled out the vase.

"Whew!" said the policeman. "That vase! Where did you get it?"

Then Benny told the whole story. He told it very well. When he had finished, the lieutenant said quickly, "Who knows you found this vase?"

"Nobody," said Benny.

"Good!" said the man. "I'm glad nobody knows that you have found the vase. The men who hid it will think it is still buried in the sandbox. Yes, I think there were two men just as you do. I think one of them hid the vase in the box of old clothes."

Benny nodded. "Then they hired Tom to buy the box and give it to them."

"Right," said the policeman. "They had to hide the vase somewhere, and your houseboat was just the place."

Jessie said, "That's why the two men were watching us when we stopped at Gull Island. They were all ready to get out of town, so they wanted to get on board and get the vase if we left the houseboat alone for a few minutes."

Benny exclaimed, "We could play a trick on them! Just let everybody know that we are going to spend the evening on land and then the men will go to the houseboat and try to get the vase back. When they get aboard, you can be in the cabin to catch them."

"That's quite a plan," said the lieutenant with a little laugh. "You can come with us. You deserve to see the end."

But Benny surprised them. He said, "No. I don't want to see those men ever again. It's just the way I feel about it."

"You don't have to," said the policeman. "Maybe your brother will go with us? We need somebody to show us where the things are on the houseboat."

"Okay," said Henry. "I'd like to."

"I know!" said Jessie. "Let's all go out on the street and let everyone know we are having supper at the Elm Tree Inn. And then we're going to the movies."

"Good!" said the policeman. "News gets around here fast. Henry, right after supper, go down to the houseboat the back way. Captain John De Rosa and I will be there. Then we'll see."

Jessie laughed. She said, "If Benny is left behind, people will think the whole family is here."

So the Aldens went out of the Elm Tree Inn,

laughing and talking. They went into every store on the street, talking together about what they were going to do. They would have supper at the inn, then go to the movies. They asked what was going on at the movies.

People smiled and told them what the picture was. By dinnertime almost every person knew the houseboat people were in town and were going to spend the evening. Who would carry the news to the men at the Princess Hotel? Nobody knew.

The Aldens had a table right in the middle of the dining room. They had a delicious dinner. Without any talk, Henry slipped out through the kitchen. He walked quickly and quietly to the houseboat. The rest of the family went to the movies and thought about the houseboat instead of the picture.

CHAPTER 10

Trapped!

When Henry stepped softly on the dock he thought that the police had not come. When he put his key in the lock he still thought that they had not come. But when he opened the door he heard a soft "Hello."

To tell the truth, Henry was very glad to hear it. There were two policemen sitting on the floor of the galley with their backs to the wall. Nobody could see them through the windows.

"Come and sit on the floor," whispered Captain De Rosa. "Sit on my other side. We want to sit nearest the door. We may have to wait a long time."

"I suppose the men may not come at all," said Henry.

"Well, maybe not," said the other policeman. "We've pulled the sandbox into the cabin. We'll let them dig a while before we jump."

"I think they'll come tonight," said Captain De Rosa. "They want to get out of this place fast."

There was no more talking. Henry could look up and see the stars out of the windows. They were bright because there were no lights and no moon. The minutes ticked away.

The water lapped gently around the boat. The night birds began to chirp and the whippoorwills sang and sang.

After a long time Henry turned his wrist over and looked at his watch. It was nine o'clock. His legs were getting stiff so he sat on one. But the policemen did not move.

Henry thought, "Maybe nobody will come tonight. Maybe they will wait until tomorrow night."

He had all sorts of ideas. "The movies will be out at ten. Suppose the men wait until ten and they meet the family coming home? That will scare them off. Suppose somebody saw me get on the boat? Suppose the two men are too strong for the police?"

Still the policemen did not move. Once Henry thought he heard a board on the dock creak. But nothing happened. Then all at once the boat moved gently. Henry could feel the policemen getting ready to stand up, but they did not move.

The boat tipped again a very little, as if a person were stepping aboard. Henry heard a key go very

softly into the lock. The door of the cabin opened. Henry could see the black shapes of two men. They stepped into the cabin and flashed a weak light toward the sandbox.

One man said crossly, "They've moved the sandbox."

"What of it?" said the other. "It's the same sandbox. Just get that vase and go!"

Both men knelt down and began to dig in the sand.

"Hold it!" cried Captain De Rosa, jumping to his feet. He turned a bright flashlight full on the two men by the sandbox.

The two men looked up with their mouths open. In an instant the two policemen had handcuffs on both of them. Then Henry was surprised to hear a car drive up.

"Our light was a signal for the car to come," explained Captain De Rosa. "We have plenty of help now." And he led the two men off the houseboat with the police lieutenant following.

"I'll lock up," said Henry. "My family can sleep here tonight without worrying about anything."

Henry had another surprise. Commander Williams

was sitting in the front seat of the car beside the police driver. "I wanted a good look at those fellows, too," he said. "Where's Benny?"

"He said this wasn't the part he wanted to see. He thinks the best ending will be feeding oats to Dolly and seeing Sam happy again."

The two handcuffed men did not make any fuss. They knew they were caught. But they began to quarrel when the station wagon started to move.

"I told you it was a dumb thing to take that vase," one said. "But you wouldn't listen. We were doing all right getting money from dumb people."

"That was my idea, too, remember! People will pay anything if you tell them their family is in trouble."

Henry thought to himself, "Sam and Jeff and the others weren't in trouble at all. But these two men are. They won't trick anybody again."

"Do you want to come to the police station with us?" asked Captain De Rosa, speaking to Henry.

"No, drop me off at the movies. I want to tell my family it's all over."

The movie had just ended. The Aldens were the

first people to come out.

"Oh, what happened, Henry?" Benny called out.

"Everything is okay," said Henry, looking at his grandfather. "Walk along to the boat and I'll tell you all about it."

Henry told the story from the beginning to the end. Then Benny said, "Oh, Grandfather, tomorrow let's float back to April Center to see Sam and Dolly!"

"We don't have to float, Ben," said Henry. "We can use the motor."

"Good, we'll get there fast," Benny said. The Aldens laughed because that sounded just like Benny.

Henry said, "How about the movie? What was it about?"

Violet looked up at Henry with a smile and said, "I haven't the slightest idea!"

That night everyone slept well on the houseboat. There was nothing to worry about.

After the houseboat was in order the next morning, Henry and Benny poled the boat toward the dock.

The Aldens bought tickets for April Center at the gate. The first person they saw was not Sam but Jeff.

He was sitting up straight in his wagon, waiting for river customers.

Benny called, "Hello, Jeff! We're back sooner than we said. It didn't take four or five days. Only two!"

"That's right," said Jeff. "I heard all about it last night." He climbed down and shook hands with Grandfather.

"You heard *last night?*" asked Henry. "It must have been late."

"Yes, it was. But I can tell you everyone around here knows it. Even before it was on the radio."

"I wonder how," said Henry.

"Well, this is a great place for getting news around," said Jeff.

"Where's Sam?" asked Benny.

"He's down at the main gate. Do you see how much better Molly looks? That's because of the oats you bought. But now I'll be able to buy all she needs. She'll look fine!"

"Good! Let's go and find Sam," Benny said.

"Have a ride!" said Jeff. "I'll be glad to take you."

The Aldens thanked him and climbed in. Down

the street went Molly. She held her head up high. People smiled as the wagon went past them. At last Molly reached the main gate.

"There's Sam!" said Benny.

Sam looked up. His face was one big smile. He pointed at Dolly. She was eating oats from a bag on her nose.

Sam said, "Dolly's fine now. And Jeff and I didn't do anything wrong, and everything is all right!"

Benny looked from Sam to Jeff and from Dolly to Molly. He said, "This is what I wanted to see—Dolly eating oats! And this is the way to end our adventure—with everybody happy!"

Jessie said, "Grandfather, don't you think our trip is really over, too?"

Mr. Alden said, "Yes, I ought to get back to work."

"I'm ready to go home," said Henry.

"Then I'll telephone Mr. Rivers," Grandfather said. But it was Mrs. Rivers who answered. She said, "I will meet you myself with my oldest boy. My husband has just gone away for the day."

The Aldens said good-bye to all their friends and

chugged away up the river in the houseboat. They looked for the last time at the green trees and the quiet water. At last they saw Mrs. Rivers and her son standing on the dock, waiting.

"What an awful time you had!" said Mrs. Rivers. "Everybody is talking about your trip and how it was spoiled."

"Oh, it wasn't spoiled," said Benny. "We had a neat time. We always have some excitement. And it all turned out well, even if those men did hide their treasure on our boat. Please don't tell Mr. Rivers the name of our boat. We'd like to have him see it himself."

Mrs. Rivers looked at the name and laughed. "No, I won't tell him," she said. "You did have some treasure aboard all the time and didn't know it."

Mrs. Rivers' son helped the Aldens take their things from the houseboat and load them in the station wagon. The drive home was a short one, and Watch was waiting for them.

After everything was unpacked, the Aldens sat on the porch. They couldn't stop talking about the houseboat.

Henry laughed and said, "Remember the day on *The James H. Alden* when Jessie lost the salt?"

And Jessie said, "Remember the day on *The Mrs. McGregor* when Ben found out why Dolly was so thin?"

Benny said, "Remember the day on the *Nedla Yrneh?* And Henry found the fish pole?"

But Violet said, "Oh, I wish we could see Mr. Rivers' face when he sees the last name for his boat!"

Really, it was too bad that nobody saw Mr. Rivers. He went down alone to look at his houseboat and get it ready for the next customer. He happened to look at the blue letters on the top and began to laugh. He laughed and laughed and slapped his knee and shook his head.

The houseboat's name was *Captain Kidd.*

"That Benny!" said Mr. Rivers. "Comical."